SUPER SIGHT FOR Seymour Bright

BY: DR. PATRICK DERESPINIS
ILLUSTRATION: JOHN EWING

Publishers Cataloging-in-Publication Data

DeRespinis, Patrick.
    Super sight for Seymour Bright / by: Dr. Patrick DeRespinis ; illustration:
John Ewing.
        p. cm.
    Summary: Eight-year-old Seymour Bright needs glasses but is afraid
of how the other children will treat him. As he discovers the benefits of
his new glasses, he also gains insight into why bullies can be unfair.
    ISBN-13: 978-1-60131-017-0
    [1. Eyeglasses--Juvenile fiction. 2. Vision--Juvenile fiction.
3. Bullies--Juvenile fiction. 4. Ophthalmologists--Juvenile fiction.
5. Optometrists--Juvenile fiction. 6. Stories in rhyme.]
    I. Ewing, John, ill. II. Title.

                                                    2007934890

To order additional copies please go to:
www.SeymourBright.com

115 Bluebill Dr.
Savannah,GA 31419
United States

This book was published with the assistance of the helpful folks at DragonPencil.

www.DragonPencil.com

Forward

As a practicing pediatric ophthalmologist I have experienced the disappointment and unhappiness in many children when they are first told they need glasses. I have also witnessed the trepidation of their parents when they first receive the "bad news." As a parent I can empathize with the family as they face unknown territory in a world where children often criticize anything that is different about their peers.

In Super Sight for Seymour Bright, Dr. DeRespinis has captured the essence of the entire experience for many first-time eyeglass wearers. The book follows Seymour's adventure from his initial eye examination to his ultimate happy acceptance of his new glasses. The excellent illustrations capture Seymour's roller coaster ride of emotions as the process of adapting to the glasses evolves.

This book is essential reading for children and parents faced with the dilemma of wearing new glasses. Dr. DeRespinis shows how a delicate situation can become a wonderfully positive experience. Super Sight for Seymour Bright belongs in the waiting areas of all ophthalmologists', optometrists' and opticians' offices. The message of the book, however, transcends the new glasses experience. The theme of tolerance and acceptance of individual differences in children makes this book a useful tool for teachers and anyone who spends a great deal of time with children.

Rudolph S. Wagner, MD
Director of Pediatric Ophthalmology
UMDNJ – New Jersey Medical School, Newark

Eight-year-old Seymour Bright
Had a problem with his sight.
Although he could not see that well,
Seymour Bright would never tell.

He could not see the birds that fly
Nor count stars in the nighttime sky.
He could not see his TV shows
Unless the screen was near his nose.

When Seymour fell and scratched his face
His parents acted with great haste.

They saw a doctor late that day
To find out what he had to say.

The doctor used a special light
To check the eyes of Seymour Bright.
The room was dark. A screen was lit
But Seymour could not read from it.

AQP
SHWL
DYRTNGO

The doctor said, "It's plain to me
That you need glasses urgently.
You cannot see signs on the street
Nor read this chart at twenty feet."

Seymour cried, "It's just not fair.
I can't wear glasses. I just don't care.
They'll hurt my ears and mess my hair.
And every kid will point and stare."

The doctor frowned and looked at him.
He spoke quite clear. His voice was grim.
"Now look here, Seymour, you see much less
Than anyone could ever guess."

"I know your parents had no clue
But surely I can fix that for you.
The glasses will improve your sight.
What's fuzzy now will soon seem bright."

"I don't like glasses, not any pair.
It's just not me and just not fair.
I don't like them. You would not dare.
They'll pinch my nose and block the air."

But Seymour soon would realize
How glasses would improve his eyes.
He saw the leaves upon the trees
And ran down stairs with greater ease.

He heard jets roar across the skies
And easily caught them with his eyes.

He now could see
while in the park

And wasn't
frightened of
the dark.

One day, a bully threw his glasses down
And broke them on the dirty ground.
That's when Seymour became aware
How kids could sometimes be unfair.

Just after the schoolyard attack,
He brought the broken glasses back.
He told the doctor what occurred
And said that everything was blurred.

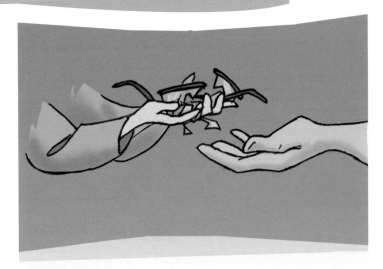

"I can't wear glasses. Aren't you aware?
My friends are treating me unfair.
I won't wear glasses. Can't you see?
These silly things are not for me."

The doctor smiled at Seymour Bright
As if he understood his plight.
"I'll make for you a brand new pair;
A super set you'll want to wear."

Seymour just didn't understand
What the doctor now had planned.
What did he mean? What did he say?
What would he give him on that day?

The glasses had a golden rim
And seemed to glow from deep within.
Seymour slid them from the case
And carefully placed them on his face.

He walked outside and looked around.
He looked straight up and then straight down.
His sight was better than before
And sharper and clearer and even more.

He saw a bumblebee buzz by
And caught each wing-beat with his eye.
Such small things he could easily see.
Each blade of grass seemed like a tree.

The next day, when he went to class,
He finished all his schoolwork fast.
With reading, writing, arithmetic;
His answers quickly seemed to click.

On the playground playing ball,
He hit each pitch beyond the wall.
He jumped real high. He climbed a tree
And ran with great agility.

Could the glasses be the key
To Seymour's new ability?
Was there magic in the frames
Or was the doctor playing games?

Seymour's friends all rubbed their eyes.
His glasses were a big surprise.
Maybe if they owned a pair
They all could see as well and share.

The bully walked toward Seymour Bright
But this time didn't want to fight.
"Hey! Who's your doctor? Please tell me!
'Cause I would also like to see."

Most kids don't always know what's right
When there's a problem with their sight.
They seem to need a helping hand
With things they cannot understand.

Seymour Bright now understood
Those things no other children could.
The glasses clearly helped him see
That kids sometimes act foolishly.

Kids tease their friends and make them cry
And call them names and even lie,
And all because they just don't know
It's differences that make them grow.

Now all the kids in Seymour's school
Will not forget this golden rule.
And you can hear in all the classes
From all those kids now wearing glasses…..

"I like my glasses. They're really cool.
They help me see when I'm in school.
I like my glasses. It's clear to see….........

What's good for Seymour is good for me."